A Brand Is Forever

A Brand Is Forever

By Ann Herbert Scott

Illustrated by
Ronald Himler

Clarion Books
New York

Clarion Books
a Houghton Mifflin Company imprint
215 Park Avenue South, New York, NY 10003.
Text copyright © 1993 by Ann Herbert Scott
Illustrations copyright © 1993 by Ronald Himler

Printed in the U.S.A.

Library of Congress Cataloging-in-Publication Data

*Scott, Ann Herbert.
A brand is forever / by Ann Herbert Scott ; illustrated
by Ronald Himler.
p.   cm.
Summary: Despite the fact that Gramp has designed and
made a special brand to be her own, Annie is distressed about
the upcoming branding of her beloved orphaned calf Doodle.
ISBN 0-395-60118-5
[1. Cattle brands—Fiction.   2. Cattle—Marking—
Fiction.   3. Ranch life—Fiction.]   I. Himler, Ronald, ill.
II. Title.
PZ7.S415Br   1993
[Fic]—dc20   91-30071
CIP
AC
BP   10   9   8   7   6   5   4   3   2   1*

With love to Leona
who has kept me going

With special thanks to the Bakers, the Rizzis, and the Thompsons of Mountain City, Nevada, Frank Dotta and the DeForests of Vinton, California, and the Marchettis of Raton, New Mexico, who showed me what branding is all about, and to other Nevadans who have given advice: Dr. Fred Anderson and Katie Scott Hess of Reno, Sharon Baker and Della Johns of Elko, Teola Manning Hall of Owyhee, Brand Inspector Dean Sheldon of Fallon, and Jack and Irene Walther of Lamoille.

I

Annie opened her blue heart locket and gently stroked the picture of her little calf, Doodle. A tuft of Doodle's silky hair slipped from the locket into her hand. She shivered. Soon it would be over. Just one more day.

Before, Annie had always looked forward to branding day. The day when all the neighbors came to give her family a hand with marking the new crop of calves. The day her dad filled the back of the pickup with pop, and the ranch women brought their favorite fancy pies, and the kids ate themselves silly.

But this time would be different. Ever since Annie had first bottle-fed her orphaned little calf back to health, she had dreaded the day her baby would be branded. And now it was tomorrow.

Humming sadly to herself, Annie rummaged in her closet for her brother Buster's old denim jacket. She was glad Buster was out with the cattle. Tough old Buster, who thought it was stupid to cry!

Annie grabbed the jacket. She'd better hurry. Gramp was probably waiting for her up at the forge and she still had the chickens to feed. She rammed her hat down over her brown braids and headed for the back door.

In the kitchen all was bustle. Annie's mother
and grandmother were cooking up a storm,
getting ready for tomorrow's branding day lunch.
Gram put down her eggbeater to give Annie a
hug.

"Cheer up, Sunshine," Gram told her. "Doodle's going to be all right. In a few days all those little calves will be chasing each other across the summer range. They'll have forgotten all about branding day."

Annie's mother looked up from a steaming kettle of spaghetti sauce. "Gramp's up at the forge already. You'd better head up there as soon as you finish your chores. He's all set to make your new brand."

Annie picked up the colander of table scraps with the bits and pieces of last night's beans and this morning's pancakes and carried it out to the yard. When she opened the door of the chicken coop, the old hens flapped their wings in alarm. Just as if she didn't feed them every morning and evening of their lives!

"Stupid chickens," Annie muttered as she fetched a bucket of fresh water to refill the empty trough.

When she grew up she knew she wouldn't raise chickens—only calves and cattle and a herd of pretty horses running free in the hills.

Annie climbed the path to the toolshed and
stopped outside. With the toe of her boot she
kicked a pebble and watched it tumble down the
brushy hill. In the corral by the barn she could see
her parents' favorite cutting horses, Ginger and

Toledo, enjoying a day off work. Far below in the meadow the mother cows were grazing with their babies. Annie couldn't tell Doodle from the other young calves cheerfully butting their heads together in the sweetness of the morning.

"I'd almost given up on you," Gramp scolded when he saw Annie in the doorway.

"I'm sorry, Gramp." Annie blinked her eyes as she came out of the bright daylight into the musty darkness of the shed. Gramp had started the fire already. Annie loved the smell of the mountain mahogany wood burning into bright coals for the forge.

Gramp hunched over the anvil, hammering away at a piece of strap iron. Annie didn't need to ask what to do. She began turning the handle of the bellows to urge on the fire. She knew the iron had to be plenty hot to be bent into a brand.

"All good things take time," said Gramp, mopping his forehead with his shirt sleeve. "And a brand is worth all the trouble it takes."

Annie nodded.

"Especially this one." Gramp went on with his hammering. "This one for you and little Doodle."

Annie turned and turned the bellows handle. She kept thinking back to the frozen February night when Gramp had first carried Doodle into the kitchen, a skinny little calf with a big wobbly head and four shaky legs. "Gramp," she asked, "do you remember the night you brought Doodle in from the barn?"

"Yep," said her grandfather.

"Remember how scared her eyes looked?"

"No wonder," said Gramp. "The little girl had just lost her mother and she was half starved to death."

"And you told me I could keep her if I could pull her through." Annie had known Gramp always sold the bull calves at the fall auction. But the heifer calves stayed at the ranch to become mother cows with little calves of their own. "I'll pull her through," Annie had promised.

"Your mother says she's never seen such a spoiled animal," Gramp said with a chuckle.

"That's because I used to sleep beside her by the stove. And then I fed her so long on the bottle."

"And because she messed up the garden where your mother had planted her daffodils."

"And she followed me wherever I went."

"Remember that day when your mother was bringing in a big load of clothes?" Gramp and Annie both began to laugh. "She tripped over Doodle taking a nap on the doorstep. She shooed that little calf all the way to the barn."

"That night I took my blankets and slept with Doodle in her stall."

Gramp hammered away at the iron. Annie turned the handle of the bellows—and turned—and turned.

"Gramp, will it hurt a lot when you brand Doodle?"

"Yep." Gramp nodded. "But it won't hurt long. Just like when Dr. Lamberts gives you a shot for the measles. For a minute there it burns like crazy. You bite your lip and try not to cry. And then it's over. That's the way it will be with Doodle."

Annie's arm was tired now from all the turning, but she was determined not to complain. "Isn't there some easier way to mark cattle?" she asked.

"Too bad there isn't," Gramp told her. "Tags fall off, paint wears out. Only the brands last as long as the cows. A brand is forever."

Annie turned and turned the bellows handle. Gramp lifted the white-hot iron from the fire and pressed the iron hard against the wall of the shed. "Here, take a look at this," he said. There beside all the other Double H family brands smoked the new brand with the A for Annie.

Gramp put his arm around Annie. "My own grandfather first made the Double H brand when he and my grandmother homesteaded this ranch. He rode his best horse all the way to the state capital to register it himself. The Double H. You can see where he first burned it there on the wall with the date beside it—1898.

"He and my grandmother were so proud. He brought her calico from town, and she made his favorite bread pudding to celebrate."

"What do the H's stand for?" Annie knew, but she wanted to hear Gramp tell it.

"The first H was for Hiram, that was my grandpa's name. And, of course, the second H is for Henderson, our family's name. He was a fine man, your great-great-grandpa. He had your love of little critters and your father's grin, and he was as tough as iron nails. The day he broke his back over beyond Lone Mountain he somehow managed to pull himself up onto his horse and ride the twelve miles home."

Annie wished she could be tough like her great-great-grandpa. Or like her mother, who wasn't afraid to break a bucking horse or kill a rattlesnake with her broom handle. Annie traced with her finger the letters of the new brand. Her own brand.

Tomorrow it would be Doodle's.

II

"I am *not* a sissy," said Annie, pushing back her
plate of breakfast biscuits and glaring at her big
brother.

"You are, too, a sissy," replied Buster, reaching
for a third helping of sausage. "Look at you, you're
almost crying right now and the branding hasn't
even started yet. I bet you won't even watch."

Annie twirled the chain of her locket and tried to think of a good thing to say. Everybody in the family knew she was so tender hearted she even shut her eyes during the sad parts on TV. "I bet I *will* watch," she muttered, hoping that saying the words out loud would help make them come true.

"Don't you remember?" Gramp asked Buster. "This year Annie's helping me with the branding fire. She's going to be right in the middle of the action."

"Some help she'll be," Buster answered. He dumped a pile of chokecherry jam on his biscuits and spread it around with the new pocket knife Gramp had given him for his birthday. "I bet Annie'll shut her eyes when you brand Doodle."

Annie wound the chain of her locket until it was tight against her throat. "Buster boy," said her mother, "if you're going to help give the calves their shots, you'd better get a move on. Just as soon as I put this ham in the oven, I'm going down to the barn with Dad. The other riders will be here before we know it."

"Annie," said her grandmother, "why don't you stay here with me? Gramp can get one of the neighbors to help with the fire, and you can lend me a hand with the ice cream."

Annie looked up at Gram. Her dear fat comfortable Gram, who always had time to tell her a story or bandage a blister or mix up a batch of cookies. "What kind of ice cream are you making?" Annie asked.

"Chocolate."

Her favorite kind. There were few things on God's green earth that Annie liked half as much as making chocolate ice cream alone with Gram.

"You can help here in the kitchen with the lunch fixings and then give Doodle a great big hug when the branding's all over."

Annie hesitated a minute, then got up from the table. "No thanks, Gram. I think I'd better give Doodle a great big hug right now."

"Don't forget your chores," called Annie's mother.

Annie turned back for the colander full of scraps.

"Chickens! Chickens! Chickens!" she grumbled. "It's branding day and I've got a calf to look after."

That morning Annie took care of the chickens in record time. She left the water bucket on the chicken coop steps and slammed the door hard. There'd be time before supper to gather the eggs.

Annie's braids sailed out behind her as she ran down the lane to the meadow where the mother cows and their calves were peacefully munching the new spring grass. Poor calves! They didn't even know what day it was.

"Come here, Doodle," Annie called as she made her way into the herd of cattle. "Come here, I have something for you."

Annie was in the middle of the herd now. All around her were cattle, the beautiful brown and white Hereford cattle that the Henderson family had been raising ever since Annie could remember.

"Come here, Doodle," Annie called. "Come here, baby." Annie ducked in and out among the mother cows and their calves. "Don't worry, Doodle," she said. "Don't worry, I'm here."

Annie herself was beginning to worry. Where could Doodle be? Could she possibly know that today the neighbors were coming to help brand the calves? Could she have decided to run away?

Or could Doodle be lost? Lost before she had a chance to be burned with the new Double H-A? Lost before the brand could tell the whole world that she belonged to Annie—forever?

"Doodle, baby, where are you?" Annie cried.

Suddenly a warm wet nose nuzzled the pocket of Annie's jeans. "Oh, Doodle," she said, laughing, and took out a handful of oats.

As Doodle munched the oats, Annie stroked the crooked white star behind the calf's great brown eyes. "My own little girl," she whispered.

Kneeling now in the pasture, Annie talked to Doodle as she picked an armload of daisies. "I'm going to make this especially for you," she told her as she began to braid the daisies into a chain. "You'll be the most beautiful calf at the branding."

Doodle sniffed the daisies, then nuzzled Annie's hand. "I wish you didn't have to be branded," Annie whispered in her ear. "I know it's going to hurt. But Gramp says the branding will just burn for a minute and then it'll all be over.

"And there's a good thing about branding." With one finger Annie drew the letters of her new Double H-A brand across Doodle's silky brown hip. "Once you've been branded with my own iron, you're never going to be lost. If you slip under the fence into the Thompsons' pasture or take off through an open gate toward Beaver Creek, someone is sure to find you and bring you home to me." Doodle nuzzled Annie again, almost as if she understood.

Just as she finished her braiding, Annie heard the ranch bell clang three times. She put the daisy chain around Doodle's neck and gave her a quick good-bye hug. "Now don't you worry," she called back to Doodle as she headed up the hill.

Under the cottonwood trees Annie's grand-mother met her with a stack of starched tablecloths.

Annie began to whistle as she shook the clean linen over the trestle tables. She remembered last year's branding day lunch. Seventeen kinds of pie! She and Buster must have tasted almost every one. And Mrs. Martinelli's brownies! Everybody in Lone Mountain said they were the best brownies in the world.

Gram came back outside with the beater from the chocolate ice cream. "See how this tastes, Annie," she said.

Annie licked the beater carefully to make the ice cream last for a long time. "It tastes terrible, Gram," she said with a grin, giving her grandmother's apron a little tug. "Has Gramp had a sample?"

"No, he's busy in the woodshed, sharpening his axe."

When the tables were all set, Annie headed for the woodshed.

"How's the fuel supply?" Gramp asked her.

"I think it'll do. I've been collecting sagebrush all week long. There's a big pile down at the branding corral."

Gramp ran his finger along the bright-edged blade of his axe. "I'm about done here," he told Annie. "Let's get the irons from the barn and head over there. I can see your mother and dad and the other riders starting to push the cattle up from the pasture."

Annie watched the cloud of dust move slowly along the lane. "Gramp, do the cows remember the branding from last year?"

"You bet they do, Annie. These mother cows don't forget."

Annie thought of Doodle, all alone without her mother. "Let's hurry," she said.

III

Outside the branding corral the mother cows were bawling, alarmed, as the riders began to separate them from their calves. Annie caught sight of her own mother astride Ginger, the best cutting horse on the ranch. But she couldn't see Doodle. Even with her new daisy chain, Doodle was lost in the crowd of frightened cattle.

"Time for us to get down to business," said Gramp. Annie brought armloads of gray, twisted sagebrush while he started a fire in the rusty old oil drum.

The little neighbor kids were taking their places on the top rails of the corral, ready to watch the day's excitement. Annie remembered all the years she'd sat there herself, watching the riders and their fancy roping, shutting her eyes when the calves were dragged to the fire.

Not today, she reminded herself. She turned back to the barrel of burning sage.

Gramp put the branding iron into the fire. "I remember my first calf," he told Annie. "My father gave her to me when I was about your age. I called her Fat Frances and she was the beginning of my whole herd."

Annie thought of Doodle. In two years she should be having a calf of her own. Maybe, if Annie were lucky, she'd even have twins. And in

the years after that there would be another calf
and another and another. Pretty soon Annie, too,
would have a herd of her own.

Just then Buster came by with the serums and syringes. "Hey," he teased, "I thought you'd be in the kitchen."

"Well, I'm not," Annie answered. "Didn't I say I'd help Gramp?"

Buster looked down at his little sister. "I bet you'll shut your eyes when Gramp brands Doodle."

"I bet I won't," said Annie.

"What'll you bet? Five dollars?" Annie had a five-dollar bill hidden under her spurs and neckerchief in her top bureau drawer, and she knew Buster had seen it.

Annie took a big breath. "I'll bet you my five dollars against your birthday knife."

Buster reached into his pocket and felt his knife, the wonderful red-handled knife with the four blades that could do almost anything.

"It's a bet," said Buster. "I know I'll win. You don't have the chance of an icicle in August."

Before Annie could answer, their dad came riding up on Toledo. "How's the branding fire?" he asked.

"Not bad," said Gramp. "The irons should be ready soon."

Annie watched the brands slowly turn from red to gold to grayish white. The calves were crowded inside the next corral while their worried mothers bellowed outside. Annie twirled her heart locket tight around her throat. She wished she could be there beside Doodle, giving her a little last-minute loving.

"Ready?" asked Annie's dad.

"Ready," Gramp answered.

"I'll be watching," called Buster.

Annie saw her dad make a loop in his lasso. A little calf came skipping toward him. With a quick throw he slipped the loop over the calf's rear heels. A minute later he was dragging the frightened animal over to the branding fire.

Little George, the cowhand from the next ranch, wrestled the calf and held his front legs tight and quiet. The calf's eyes bulged with fear. Annie was glad it wasn't Doodle. Buster grabbed the syringes and gave the calf its shots while Gramp's friend Old Nicholas cut a wedge into the middle of the calf's left ear, their ranch's own special mark.

Gramp reached into the fire and pulled out one of the old branding irons. Carefully, he pressed it to the calf's hip. As it touched, there was a sizzling sound, then a puff of smoke and the stink of burning hair. Annie shivered, but she kept her eyes wide open.

The calf struggled to his feet and bounded off to find his mother. Gramp was right. It only did take a minute.

"Is it hard to make a good brand?" Annie asked.

"There's quite a trick to it," Gramp answered. "If you go too deep, you ruin the calf's hide. If you're not deep enough, the brand won't last. You have to catch it just right."

The calves came fast now. Annie's mother and dad and three other ranchers took turns lassoing. Sometimes their ropes fell exactly in place. Sometimes they missed and the little calves kicked up their heels and ran around the corral. At those times Annie wanted to clap her hands and cheer for the calves. But she saw that the ropers always caught up with them in the end.

On the ground the branding crew worked together, calf after calf after calf. The bucket of ear wedges beside Old Nicholas gradually began to fill.

Annie stayed close to her grandfather, feeding the fire and keeping an eye out for Doodle and her daisy necklace. "Gramp," she asked, "why does a calf need an earmark when it's already got a brand?"

"It's easy to ask that today when you're watching the calves one by one. But think about looking for a lost cow in a crowded bunch of cattle. Maybe you can see her head better than her hip. Or maybe it's snowing and there's ice caked so thick on her brand that it's hard to make out. Earmarks come in handy lots of times. You'll notice all the neighbor ranches use them, too."

"Hey, look who's here!" shouted Annie's mother. There, dragging at the end of her rope, was the little calf with the crooked star.

Doodle's daisy necklace was wilted now, and her eyes were big with fright. She didn't even know Annie was nearby. "I'm right here, baby," Annie called to her. But Doodle didn't seem to hear.

Annie's hand trembled as she gave Gramp the iron with the Double H-A. More than anything in the world she wanted to shut her eyes until the branding was over. But she'd made a bet and she knew Buster was watching. "It'll be over in a minute, Doodle," she called.

Doodle lay still. Quickly Old Nicholas cut a
notch in her ear and Buster stuck in the syringes.
Annie's eyes were filled with tears as Gramp
touched her new brand to Doodle's hip. The iron
hissed as it burned the Double H-A into Doodle's
silky hide. Tears rolled down Annie's cheeks. But
she didn't shut her eyes. Not even for a second.

Then it was over. Dazed, Doodle pulled herself to her feet. With a shake of her head she put up her tail and scampered off. Annie looked over at Buster, but he was busy refilling the syringes.

Annie wished she could chase after Doodle to comfort her, but she knew there was still work to do. With a sigh she loaded more sagebrush on the fire.

Finally, her dad yelled, "Here come the last of them!" Soon he was handing out cans of pop from the back of the pickup.

Annie walked over to where Buster was packing up the syringes. "I never shut my eyes once," she told him.

"I know, I kept watching you." Buster slowly reached into his jeans pocket for the red-handled knife. "I guess you won fair and square."

Annie smiled. "I'll tell you what," she said. "Why don't you do my chores for a month and keep your old knife? I want to go find Doodle."

"O.K. by me." Buster shrugged in relief.

"You can start tonight by feeding the chickens." Annie laughed as she grabbed a can of pop and hurried off.

Annie ran back to the house where the men were beginning to wash up and the ranch women were fetching the hot dishes for the lunch. Just then her grandmother came through the kitchen door carrying a big blue and white platter. "I don't suppose you'd be interested in one of Mrs. Martinelli's brownies?" she asked Annie.

"How about two? One for me and one for Doodle."

Stuffing one brownie in her mouth and the other in her shirt pocket, Annie headed for the pasture. There at the fence waiting for her was Doodle.

Annie threw her arms around Doodle's neck. "My dear brave Doodle," she told her. "My own brave little Doodle."

Doodle nuzzled the brownie in Annie's pocket.

"It's all yours." Annie smiled. Then she began to chuckle to herself. "And my chores are all Buster's."

Tenderly Annie stroked Doodle's hip near the burnt brown letters of the Double H-A. "No matter what happens," she whispered to Doodle, "you'll always belong to me. Remember, a brand is forever."

A NOTE ON BRANDING

The brand is the home address label for the cow who grazes on the unfenced open range. As far back as four thousand years ago, the owners of cattle and other animals burned them with special designs to prevent their being lost or stolen. Wall paintings on early Egyptian tombs show pictures of oxen being branded much as cattle are branded today.

Cattle branding was pioneered by the Spanish explorers who brought the first cattle and horses to the Western Hemisphere in the sixteenth century. Later, cattle owners from coast to coast—English settlers in the Colonies and Spanish missions in California—used brands to identify their property. Brands became an important part of the cattle business in the vast open spaces of the West.

Many brands are little pictures: ⊬ "Pitchfork," ⋏ "Sunrise," and ⊿ "Stirrup." Others are made up of letters or numbers. T reads, simply, "T." Add legs ⅀ and it becomes a "Walking T." Add wings T and it's a "Flying T," or lying down ⊢ it's a "Lazy T." Any letter hanging by its top "swings," as in the "Swinging M" M , or when placed on part of a circle it "rocks," as in "Rocking M" M . When two letters are the same, they are "double," as in Annie's family brand the "Double H." Brands are read from left to right, ⋕⋏ "Double H A"; from top to bottom, B̄Q̄ "Barbecue"; and from outside to inside, ◈ "Diamond C."

In the United States today each brand must be officially registered with the owner's county or state government and listed in the local brand book. No two similar brands can be registered in the same area. Registration gives the owner the exclusive right to burn a particular design on a particular part of the animal, left or right hip or rib. Families treasure their own brands and pass them down from generation to generation.